MICE

of the

HERRING BONE

TIM DAVIS

Bob Jones University Press, Greenville, South Carolina 29614

Library of Congress Cataloging-in-Publication Data

Davis, Tim.
    Mice of the Herring Bone / written and illustrated by Tim Davis.

    Summary: After stowing away on a pirate ship manned by nasty
sea dogs, mice Charles and Oliver become involved in their plot to
attack a ship of cats and steal a load of sunken treasure belonging to
the Queen of England.
        ISBN 0-89084-626-X
        [1. Pirates—Fiction. 2. Buried treasure—Fiction. 3. Mice—
Fiction. 4. Dogs—Fiction. 5. Cats—Fiction.] I. Title.
PZ7.D3179Mi 1992
[Fic]—dc20   92-11425
                                                              CIP
                                                               AC

Mice of the Herring Bone

Edited by Katherine Mahler

Cover and illustrations by Tim Davis

© 1992 Bob Jones University Press
Greenville, South Carolina 29614

ISBN 0-89084-626-x

20   19   18   17   16   15   14   13   12   11   10   9   8

To my wife, Becky,
who showed me that writing
can be fun
and
to my pet, Kiki,
who showed me that cats
can be good guys, sometimes

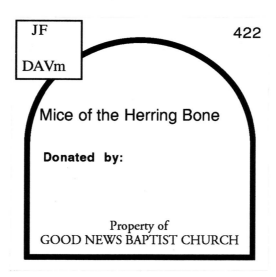

Contents

Chapter One
The Pirate Ship

Two mice scampered across
the deck of the *Herring Bone*.
They slipped into the shadows
under the rail and stopped to
listen. All was still.

Oliver moaned. "Oooh, if
we ever get back to London,
I'll never go near the docks again."

"Now cheer up, old fellow,"
Charles said. "You know it was all
an accident. I've told you time
and time again how sorry I am
about the whole mess.

Besides, who was the one who fussed about an empty stomach?"

"Shh—." Oliver looked nervously up and down the deck, but the ship still rocked quietly at anchor. "Well," he sighed. "The next time you sneak into a barrel of meal, don't expect me to follow you."

"Of course I had no idea they'd load our barrel onto a ship. Especially *this* ship." Charles whisked under the rail to gaze at the island nearby.

"So this is San Gato. Isn't it a pretty sight?" The island had a tall mountain surrounded by palm trees. It looked silver in the moonlight.

"Well, 'tain't London, but it's okay," said Oliver. "I imagine the island's got a good many nuts and berries around."

Charles shook his head. "Really, Oliver, is that all you think about?" But he had to smile at his chubby friend. "I'm getting tired of pirate's food too. Let's try the captain's cabin again. He seems to eat better than most."

The two mice scrambled along the rail and crossed the deck. They squeezed under the door into the captain's cabin. It was a small room, but finer than any of the others.

Best of all, the captain had filled it with all sorts of seaman's knickknacks. Charles's favorite was a small ship inside a long glass bottle.

It was named the *Herring Bone,*
a perfect model of the real ship itself.

"I never could figure out how
those things get into bottles," said
Oliver. He started nibbling on a crumb.
Charles was about to join him when
a slit of light gleamed under the door.

Voices murmured outside, and feet
shuffled. Something went *ker-thonk,*
ker-thonk. Charles and Oliver sped
to a shadowy corner.

"Well, mates," growled a voice.
"Let's have our talk in here."
The door opened. An old bulldog
with a black patch over one eye
strutted into the room. Charles
had heard that he was the meanest
pirate on the ship. Captain Crag.

Behind him trotted the
first mate, Big Tom, a dog with
shaggy, brown fur and a bad temper.
Then came O'Grady. At the sight
of the wooden-legged mutt,
Charles squeezed further into his
corner. Maybe the sharp-eyed parrot on
O'Grady's shoulder wouldn't spot
them.

Captain Crag set the lantern down
on the table, and all three dogs
crouched around it.

"Well, Cap'n," started O'Grady.
"I smells a nasty piece o' business,
us bein' roused up fer a secret chat.
Hee, hee. What'll it be? A cat what
needs drownin'?"

"Caw," squawked Barnacle,
the parrot.

The bulldog captain scratched his hairy chin. "Yer brain might be disjointed, O'Grady, but you sure has a good heart." Then he smiled. "It's better than that, mates. What d'you think of stealin' treasure from a ship full of cats?"

Tom hunched down and whispered, "Stealin' treasure, Cap'n?"

"Aye, mateys," replied Crag. "And there's plenty of it too."

"Well, blow me down." O'Grady slapped his wooden leg. "An' cats fer drownin' too? Hee, hee!"

Big Tom kicked him. "Quit yer noise. Want to stir up everybody afore it's time?"

The captain went on. "There's a
ship anchored on the other side of the
island. Flyin' the Queen's flag. Far
as I can tell, she ain't seen us yet.
'Tis the *Nine Lives*."

Charles exchanged a glance
with Oliver. A ship full of
cats? That sounded even worse
than pirates.

But O'Grady was smiling.
His eyes bulged out. "Oooh. . . !"

"Now listen." Captain Crag
frowned at him and went on.
"I heard 'bout that *Nine Lives*.
'Twas sent here by the Queen.
Her ship, the *Klondike*,
sank in a storm off San Gato
just a few months ago. An' it had
a cargo of gold and precious jewels."

Big Tom grinned. "So you'll let
them cats bring up the treasure.
Then we steals it from 'em?"

"Aye, that's it, Tom,"
replied Captain Crag.

"Caw," squawked the parrot.
"Gold!"

Tom's grin faded. "But Cap'n, how's we gonna know when they find the treasure?"

"Well, that's whar you two comes in," said the captain.

"Those cats, they probably does a lot of talking, as cats do. So tonight you two row over there in the skiff. It's so small, no one will notice you aside thar ship. One of these nights, you'll hear that they've found the treasure."

Big Tom and O'Grady stared at him. But the captain was already standing up. "You'd best get started now, mateys, afore the moon gits any higher."

Captain Crag picked up the lantern from the table. O'Grady grabbed a big bottle of soda water from the shelf, and Big Tom followed them out of the room.

Charles and Oliver stood frozen in the shadows.

"Phew, I almost lost my appetite," sighed Oliver. "Especially with that wooden-legged monster here."

"Well, finish up your crumb and let's get going," said Charles.

"Going? Where?"

"To get onto that boat, of course," answered Charles. "We've got to warn those cats somehow."

"Warn the *cats*? Even
if they are the Queen's sailors,
and they're *supposed* to be
fed well—" Oliver shook his head.
"Oh, no, not me!"

"What are you—a mouse or a flea?
That treasure belongs to the
Queen." Charles stood up straight
and tall. "It's only the right thing
to do! Now come along."

Charles grabbed his
friend's hand and pulled him
out the door. Together
they crept from shadow to shadow
toward the skiff.

Chapter Two
Stowaways

"Now," whispered Charles.
Oliver followed, his tail dragging.
The two mice slipped into the little
boat just as Captain Crag began
cranking it down into the water.

Charles didn't like the way the
waves slapped against the skiff.
But he held onto a rusty nail and sent
Oliver a weak grin. Big Tom and O'Grady
loosened the ropes and signaled to the
captain above them.

"Caw," said Barnacle.

"Keep yer squawkin' parrot quiet!" muttered Big Tom.

The bird flapped over and beat his wings on Tom's nose. "Hee, hee!" laughed O'Grady.

"Git him offa me, O'Grady," growled Tom, "afore I wring his neck."

"Hee, hee, that'll be enough, Barney." O'Grady took a swig of his soda water. "Big Tom's a mighty bad sport. Better leave 'im be."

The skiff slipped out into the moonlight. As it rounded the island, Charles peered through a crack. The *Nine Lives* lay several yards ahead. Her sails were rolled up, and her golden lanterns shone across the waves.

O'Grady seemed to know just where to go. He steered the skiff into the wide shadow cast by the ship and let it drift below an open window. They waited in the darkness, barely rippling the water.

Before long Charles heard voices. He nudged his shivering friend.

"Come in," a deep, purring sort of voice said. "Ah, Mr. Calico, please be seated."

"Thank you, Admiral."

"So tell me, Mr. Calico, do you believe we're getting any closer to the *Klondike*?"

"Well, sir, I'd indeed like to think so, though we haven't come up with a stitch of gold yet, sir."

"Ah, well," sighed the Admiral. "As they say, a stitch in time saves nine. Perhaps in this case, the *Nine Lives*. Ha, ha, ha."

"Yes, sir." Mr. Calico's voice was polite.

The Admiral went on. "I do hate to disappoint our Queen. Put some more men on the job and offer a reward. Start searching again first thing tomorrow morning."

"Yes, sir, that we will, sir."

O'Grady giggled as they sat outside in the shadows.

"Shhh." Big Tom pushed off from the ship.

"I was only thinkin' ahead," whispered O'Grady. He took a long drink of soda water.

Just then Charles saw the parrot turn its head. Those beady eyes were staring at something.

Oh, no, he thought. We'd better—

But Barney was already flapping down toward them. "Caw."

"Keep yer half-wit bird still," scolded Tom in a hoarse whisper. "He'll give us away."

"Oliver, jump for it," cried Charles. Oliver squeaked in alarm. But the parrot had already snatched them up in its claws.

"Why lookie what Barney's caught himself, now. Stowaways!" O'Grady's eyes gleamed. "Hee, hee, hee!"

Big Tom eyed the two mice, looking interested. "Stowaways?"

Charles wondered if they would make even one mouthful for the huge dog.

"Why, we gotta treat our mousey guests to some soda water, ain't we, Tom?" whispered O'Grady. "Give 'em to me, Barney."

He plucked Charles and Oliver from Barney's claws and stuffed them into his half-empty bottle. Then he corked it shut and hurled it over the water.

"Enjoy yer drink, mateys."

Ker-plop.
The bottle dropped into the sea
and began to sink.

Inside, Oliver splashed frantically
in the soda water. "Help!" he cried.
"Help! Help!"

"Stop it, Oliver," scolded
Charles, bobbing alongside.
"You're just making a lot of fizz,
and we haven't time for that."

"What are we going to do?!"

"Why, we've got to get that cork
out, of course, and swim back to the
surface. Now you do just what I do."

Charles leaned to one side, and so
did Oliver. The bottle flipped over.

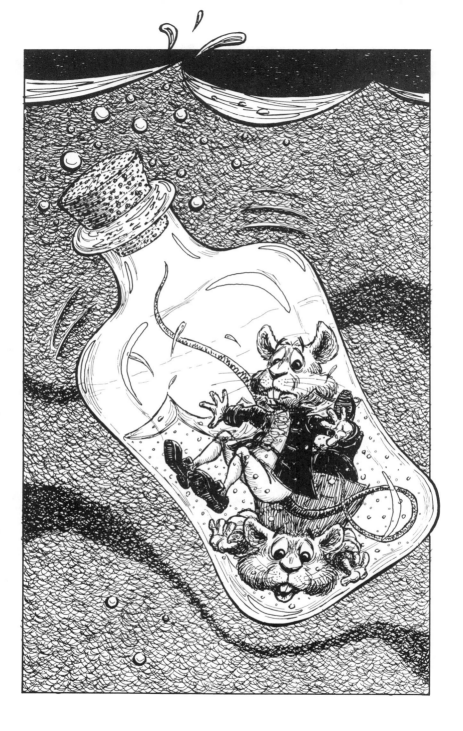

Immediately they were covered
with soda water, but they landed
on the cork face down.

"P-p-push-sh," bubbled Charles.
He braced himself in the bottle's neck
and thrust downward with all his might.
Oliver joined him in the struggle, but
it was hard getting leverage in such
tight quarters.

Soon Charles was out of breath, and
both had to bob up for air. The bottle
flipped over again, splashing a great
deal of soda water up Oliver's nose. He
choked and wheezed. At last he sobbed,
"It's no use. We're sunk."

Chink. Charles cocked his head.
"My friend," he said,
"it sounds as if we just hit bottom."

He turned and glanced through the glass. "Look, Oliver! Look where we've landed!"

"Probably someplace terrible. On an octopus?"

"No, it's gold! The treasure! We've found the wreck of the *Klondike*!" Charles dove down through the soda water for a closer look.

Above him, Oliver muttered, "A lot of good it's going to do us— or the Queen, either."

Charles peered through the thick glass at the bottom of the bottle. Gold coins. Gold rings. Gold necklaces. What a fortune!

He bobbed back up to tell Oliver.
But his friend had turned pale.
He looked almost white.

"Really, Oliver, what is it?"
asked Charles. He stared out into the
water, and his jaw dropped open.
A shark? Yes. And it was coming
right at them.

Chapter Three
Cats and Mice

The great fish shot toward the
bottle, its open mouth like a giant red
cave. Oliver let out a terrified squeak
as the shark's mighty jaws closed around
their bottle.

The bottle shattered, and several
jagged pieces of glass flew into
the shark's mouth. The huge fish choked
and thrashed about in the water.
The next thing they knew, Charles
and Oliver were out of the bottle
and swimming for their lives.

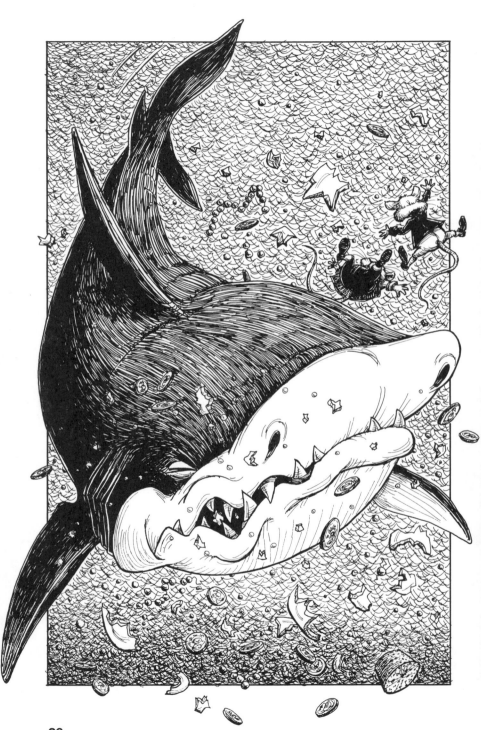

The two mice struggled toward the
surface. Charles began to get dizzy.
He saw that Oliver was sinking,
and he grabbed for his friend's paw.
He pulled and kicked. He thrust
himself upward with the last
of his strength.

With one last stroke, Charles
reached the surface, still clutching
Oliver's paw. He felt a gentle breeze
on his face. And there was the moon above
them! He coughed, and thankfully filled
his aching lungs with air.

Oliver was still coughing and
sputtering. "Thanks, pal," he said.

"Think nothing of it, old fellow,"
said Charles. "I couldn't go treasure
hunting without you, could I?"

"No, I suppose not."
Oliver stopped to cough again.
"Though I might be better off
if you did."

Charles laughed, and they set off
for the *Nine Lives*, several yards
away.

"From mad dogs to civilized
cats . . ." muttered Oliver. "I suppose
it's an improvement. One thing's
certain—I'll sink to the bottom if we
stay in the water much longer.
Honestly, I feel as if I've gained a
bundle of weight today."

"And you were complaining about
the food?"

Oliver patted at his belly.
"Hey, wha-a-?"

"What is it, Ollie?"

"What's this? Something's hooked onto my pants." Oliver pulled up the "something" and held it above the water. There, sparkling in the moonlight, was a large golden earring.

"Why, Oliver, you've brought up some treasure with you!"

"Well, look at that, will you? No wonder I felt so heavy— it looks like solid gold!"

It seemed like a long time later that they reached the *Nine Lives*.

"Whew!" Oliver grabbed onto the ship's rudder. "I thought my legs were going to drop off."

"It's been quite a long swim," agreed Charles.

"Too long," panted Oliver. "Even a ship full of cats looks good to me now."

The two friends climbed up onto a small ledge just below a window. There they rested, letting their clothes dry out. Charles wrapped the golden earring in his vest, and they both fell asleep.

Charles awoke suddenly at the sound of a voice. It came from the cabin above their ledge.

"Will there be anything else, Admiral?"

"Hmmm, perhaps so, Mr. Calico.

Would you kindly bring me a mug of warm milk before I retire?"

"Yes, sir, Admiral Winchester."

The Admiral set his lantern on the windowsill. He seemed to be getting ready for bed, all the while humming a cheery tune.

"He sounds like a pleasant enough chap," whispered Charles, "for a cat. I say, let's show him that golden earring and have a chat with the fellow. After all, he's the Queen's man, so to speak."

"Don't you think we ought to wait until he gets some warm milk in his stomach first?" asked Oliver. "I mean, maybe then he'd be too full to eat us."

"Oliver, now's as good a time as any. Besides, what cat would stuff himself with mice when warm milk is on the way?"

"I guess you're right." But Oliver hesitated. "Maybe I should wait out here for you.

Uh—you have such a way with words—I'd be no help at all."

Charles didn't like the idea of going in alone, but he clutched the golden earring and climbed across the window ledge. He stood there by the lantern and cleared his throat. "Ahem. Excuse me, sir."

The cat kept right on humming, getting ready for bed.

Charles tried again. "Ahem." Once more his small voice went unnoticed. Then an idea came to him. He waved his hand back and forth in front of the lantern. A strange shadow flitted across the room.

"Eeyow!" The startled cat jumped right out of his bedroom slippers.

Charles said timidly,
"Uh, excuse me, sir."

The Admiral jerked around.
His face looked as if he were
expecting a ghost. "A mouse?"
he gasped.

Charles swallowed hard. "At your
service, sir. And I'm frightfully sorry
if I startled you."

"What? Me, startled? Ha, ha."
The Admiral took a while to put on
his bedroom slippers again.

Then his eyes narrowed
suspiciously. He stepped closer
to the windowsill. "But I
just might ask what business a
mouse has—without orders—
on Her Majesty's Ship,
the *Nine Lives*."

Chapter Four
Safe or Sorry?

Charles backed up a step.
"Well, s-sir, I have some g-good
news and—and some bad news—"

He swallowed hard as the Admiral
came within a paw's reach of him.
"And I'm sure that if you listen,
it would be better—er—much better
than e-eating a poor m-mouse like me."

The Admiral smiled. "Rest
assured, good fellow. I am well fed in
the Queen's service and will gladly
refrain from eating you. As they say,
'Feed the cat, save the mouse.' Ha, ha."

Charles sighed in relief.
He pulled out the golden earring
and handed it to the Admiral.
Then he hopped onto the table
and told Admiral Winchester the
reason for his strange visit.

Before long they were
interrupted by Mr. Calico,
who carried the Admiral's milk.

"Yes, come in, Mr. Calico."

The sailor set the mug down.
He raised one eyebrow at the sight
of a mouse on the table.

Admiral Winchester turned to him.
"Mr. Calico, perhaps you are wondering
about this rather strange
conversation."

"Oh, not at all, sir."

"You *do* frustrate me, Mr. Calico." The Admiral smiled at Charles. "I believe that Mr. Calico is the least curious of all cats!"

"Mr. Calico, this mouse has some most interesting news. Apparently we are being watched by sea dogs on the other side of the island."

"Sea dogs?"

"Yes, the sea dogs of the *Herring Bone.* Pirates, I believe you said—" The Admiral turned to Charles.

"Quite correct. A nasty lot," said Charles.

"These scoundrels are lurking behind San Gato," the Admiral continued.

They are waiting for the treasure
to come on board before they—"

Another enormous shadow loomed
across the wall. "Eeyow!" shrieked the
Admiral.

"Oliver!" squeaked Charles.

The plump mouse stood on the window
ledge, looking timid. "Nice place you
have here, Mr. Admiral, sir."

Quickly Charles introduced Oliver,
and his friend scrambled down to join him
on the table. Admiral Winchester took a
long drink of his warm milk.

Then he continued.
"As I was saying, Mr. Calico,
as soon as we bring up the gold,
those pirates will be upon us."

"But we are safe enough
until we have found the treasure?"
asked Mr. Calico.

The Admiral pulled the golden
earring out of his vest pocket.
"Mr. Calico, we *have* found
the treasure."

Now even Mr. Calico looked
curious. "Where, sir?"

"Our two small friends happened
upon it not three hundred yards from
this spot," the Admiral said.

He narrowed his eyes. "And,
Mr. Calico, I believe we should
make every effort to bring that
treasure up *tonight*."

Everyone on the crew agreed with Admiral Winchester. All of them wanted to help rescue the Queen's treasure. And none of them wanted to tangle with pirate sea dogs. If they could just pick up the treasure that night, they could slip away unnoticed.

The Admiral gathered his crew in a dimly lit cabin below deck. He spoke in a whisper. "Remember, my good fellows—we must do this job in silence. Let each cat go about his task, as it were, as quietly as a mouse."

The Admiral nodded at Charles and Oliver, then he chuckled. The cats nodded too, with polite chuckles all around.

"Well, then," he continued. "Are there any questions?"

"Aye, forgive me fer askin'," said one old sailor. "But just how are we going to latch onto this treasure in the middle of the night so's we kin pull it up to the ship?"

"Ah, yes." The Admiral smiled. "I knew I'd forgotten something. Our brave friends here, Charles and Oliver, have kindly agreed to do the special sort of diving—"

"We're going to do *what*?" Oliver whispered hoarsely to Charles.

Chapter Five
Sunken Treasure

"Er, yes, old fellow," said Charles.
"I told the Admiral we'd do that.
Sorry, I forgot to mention it—"

"We're going under water again?"
moaned Oliver. "Ohhh . . . I hope
that shark doesn't know we're coming."

Soon everything was ready.
Several cats manned ropes and pulleys.
Others prepared to lower the ship's
small skiff into the water.
They worked silently, speaking in
whispers, with only the moon
to give them light.

Oliver watched while Charles talked with Admiral Winchester and Mr. Calico. "—A square knot, you say?"

"That's right," replied the mate. "A square knot should do the trick. Then one yank, and we'll bring you up. We can handle it from there."

"Sounds simple enough," replied Charles.

"Ah, here comes the diving chamber now," exclaimed the Admiral.

Three cats were lifting a heavy iron cannon barrel out of the hatch.

"You mean they're going to shoot us under the water? Like cannonballs?" squeaked Oliver.

"Oh, Oliver, don't be silly.
They're going to lower it under water
from pulleys on the skiff," explained Charles.
"A big air bubble will be trapped inside the
cannon barrel. We'll stay inside there, and
we'll signal them with ropes until they
get over the sunken treasure."

Charles smiled at him. "Then
we'll tie the ropes to the treasure.
They'll bring us up for air and haul
up the treasure too. Then we'll go
down and find some more, and so on,
until we have it all!"

Charles paused. "Isn't it clever?"

Oliver looked at him. "Are you
sure a *cat* couldn't fit in that
cannon barrel instead?"

Charles rolled his eyes and sighed. "Oh, Oliver."

The *Nine Lives* pulled up anchor. It drifted as close as possible to the place where Charles remembered seeing the treasure. Then the skiff was lowered to the water with the cannon barrel hanging from a pulley on the side.

"Here we go," said Charles. Suddenly he felt very solemn.

The two mice climbed into the cannon barrel, carrying a small candle. It would be their only light under the deep, dark sea. Oliver and Charles gave the "ready" signal and braced themselves for the descent.

Pulleys cranked. Water gurgled. Sloshed. Bubbled. Down and down they went. Inside the barrel, water crept up toward their feet. Finally Charles dipped his face under the water. "Oliver, take a look! I think I see something over on the left."

Oliver stuck his face into the water, pulled it out, and nodded at Charles.

"That's it," cried Charles. "The very same treasure chest!" He jerked the rope four times, the signal to move left. Gradually the skiff above them turned into position, just a foot or so from the treasure chest.

Oliver jerked the rope twice. Then Charles grabbed it, took another deep breath, and dove down onto the chest.

He held onto a handle with one foot and tied a perfect square knot around it.

Then he came up into the barrel for air, took another rope, and tied it around the lock. Soon the sunken chest was tied with all four ropes. Charles gave one last yank on the rope and swam back up to the cannon barrel.

Before long, the two mice were back in the skiff. They rested while the crew cranked up the treasure. "Never seen a better square knot," Mr. Calico said. "You two did a fine job."

"Oh, it was nothing," Oliver answered. "Charles is the best in the business when it comes to tying knots." Then he busied himself with the candle.

Soon they were ready to dive again. There was a great deal of treasure. Some of the gold was in boxes, more was in chests, and many coins and gems simply lay scattered along in the sand. After several more dives, it seemed that they had brought up just about everything.

Charles noticed that the sky was beginning to lighten.

Mr. Calico took hold of the skiff's oars. "We just got a signal from the *Nine Lives* —time to go in."

"I'm all for that," sighed Charles.

"Me, too," moaned Oliver. "What's for breakfast?"

Mr. Calico smiled. "Anything you like. How about some bread and cheese?"

Oliver closed his eyes and leaned back with a smile. The cats rowed the little boat over to the ship, helped by a rather stiff breeze.

All the while, Mr. Calico kept an anxious eye on the eastern sky. It was growing pinker by the minute. Charles heard him mutter, "Yes, it's certainly time to get going."

Chapter Six
Stormy Seas

Quickly the treasure was loaded and
tied down on board the *Nine Lives*.
The Admiral and his crew expected
to slip away before daybreak.
There was no time to lose.

They pulled up the ship's anchor.
The sails whipped open in the wind,
and the *Nine Lives* began its escape.

Charles gave a sigh of relief.
Then he saw Mr. Calico's face.
What was bothering the first mate?

Admiral Winchester was looking
grim too. *"Red sky in morning,
sailors take warning,* eh, Mr. Calico?"

"Yes, sir, Admiral. That wind's
kicking up mighty strong. Looks
like we're headed for a storm."

"I'm afraid you're right, Mr.
Calico." The Admiral gazed at the dark
gray clouds ahead. "How long do you
think we can tack into this wind?"

"She's doing fine now,"
said the cat. "But I hope that wind
doesn't get much stronger. It'll
blow us right back to San Gato."

At last they all sat down at
the Admiral's table to enjoy
a much needed meal.

The cats told Charles and Oliver how brave they had been in helping with the *Klondike*'s sunken treasure.

Oliver gave a shrug. "Really, it was nothing. We rather like adventure."

"Oh, yes," added Charles. "It's hard to keep Oliver *out* of a dangerous place!"

By the end of the meal, clouds had covered the newly risen sun. The sea was gray and foamy, and spray swept over the deck. Mr. Calico stared ahead, sizing up the storm.

Suddenly a cry rang from the stern. "Ship ahoy! Ship ahoy!"

Mr. Calico gasped. "The pirates! They must have figured out that we found the Queen's treasure."

Pow! A cannon blasted across the waves. An iron ball splashed into the sea. But it was only a few yards short of the *Nine Lives*.

"Next they'll be close enough to hit the deck." The Admiral shouted orders above the howling wind. "Prepare the cannons to return fire."

The crew rushed to the cannons. But waves had washed over their powder keg. The gunpowder was ruined.

"And look, sir," said Mr. Calico, pointing to the creaking masts. "That wind's going to snap this ship in two before long."

The Admiral braced himself as another wave splashed across the deck. "You're right. Take down the sails."

"Cast the anchor," he shouted.
"Surely the *Herring Bone* will
have to do the same."

But the wind had swept the
pirate ship much too close.

Pow! Bang! The pirates blasted
the deck of the *Nine Lives*. The
cats couldn't shoot back. All they
could do was dodge the iron balls and
check for damage. Before long the whole
crew was drenched and weary.

In his cabin, Admiral Winchester
met with Mr. Calico and the two mice.
They stared at the maps and charts on
the table. Was there any way of escape?

Mr. Calico frowned. "Sir, we
could ram directly into them.

But then we'd surely wreck
on the rocks of the island."

The Admiral rubbed his eyes.
Charles and Oliver hopped onto the map
to study it more closely.

Bam! Another cannonball smashed
onto the deck. Then came the sound of
creaking, splintering planks.

"I don't know how many more lives
this ship has left in her," sighed the
Admiral. "Soon we'll be carrying more
iron than gold!"

Bang! A shot hit right above
the cabin. The window shutters snapped
wide open, and wind blasted into the
room. Maps, charts, and papers sailed
out the window.

Charles and Oliver grabbed onto the
map as it lifted them off the table.
Out the window they flew, across the
stormy waves of the sea.

Chapter Seven
Ship to Ship

Charles and Oliver could not even
squeak. The map blew high above the
foaming waves. They felt dizzy
as it flitted and fluttered,
but they dared not let go.

Suddenly, *wham!* The
map and its passengers smacked
hard against something.
Charles poked his head up.
Ropes. The wind had wrapped
the map around a network of ropes.

Charles shook himself back to his
senses. "Oliver," he cried. "Grab
onto the rigging before the wind rips
this map to shreds!"

Oliver snatched at the rope.
A minute later, the map tore
and blew into the sea.
"Ooooo, Charles," he moaned,
"where are we?"

Charles had to shout above the
wind. "I'm afraid we're back on the
Herring Bone!"

"The *Herring Bone* again?"
groaned Oliver. "Let's stay clear of
that crazy pirate with the wooden
leg!"

Charles nodded, then he
waved at Oliver to follow him.
They crept down the rigging toward
the deck. Below, the sea dogs
were busy loading their cannons and
blasting at the *Nine Lives.*

The mice waited with pounding
hearts. When no one was watching,
they hopped onto the deck
and scurried into the shadows.
For now, they were safe.

"Fire!" shouted one of the
pirates. *Bang, bang, bang!*
Three cannonballs blazed across the
water toward the helpless ship.

"They ain't fired back one shot!"
snarled one dog. "Why don't they
jest give up?"

"Ha!" growled another. He was
loading a cannon. "They won't give up
if they knows what's good for 'em."

Soon the pirates began making jokes
about the cats. Would they be dumb enough
to surrender?

All the while, the cannons kept
firing ball after ball at the *Nine Lives*.
Both ships rocked in the howling storm.

The mice listened from the shadows.
"Oliver, we've simply got to *do*
something," exclaimed Charles.

"Most certainly," agreed his
chubby friend. "But what?"

Charles thought hard. Harder than
a mouse had ever thought before.
Suddenly, it came to him.

"We'll chew the anchor
loose," he said.

"That's it!" squeaked Oliver.
"Nobody will be paying any attention.
And it's way down in the hold!"

"Right," agreed Charles. "While they're busy on deck shooting, we'll be busy downstairs chewing!"

"And as soon as that rope lets loose, the wind will drive the ship out of range!" Oliver grinned.

"But—" Charles stopped short.

"What's the matter, old fellow?"

"What you just said. The wind will drive us right into San Gato."

"Oh." Oliver's whiskers twitched. "I guess we'll be—shipwrecked— then, won't we?"

"I guess so."

The two mice gazed at each other for a moment. Finally Oliver spoke up.

"It's either we get shipwrecked on the *Herring Bone*, or the *Nine Lives* gets blasted to splinters, eh?"

"That's what it looks like."

"Hmmmm." Oliver paused again. "Let's go then, old fellow. Looks like we've got some ropes to chew."

Charles smiled and patted his friend on the back. "You're right. We'll do our best for the Queen."

The two mice waited their chance and then darted from their hiding place. They dodged the pirates' feet, skittered across the slippery deck, and slid down into the ship's hold. Finally they reached a small room deep inside the *Herring Bone*. Coiled ropes were heaped all over the floor.

One rope was wound around a large iron crank. It disappeared through a small, iron-rimmed hole in the side of the ship.

"That's it," squeaked Charles. "The anchor rope."

"But look! It must be two inches thick," exclaimed Oliver.

"Well, I hope you're good and hungry, old fellow," said Charles. "Let's go to it." He began to gnaw at the heavy rope.

Before long they heard a familiar sound just above them.

Ker-thonk, ker-thonk.

"O'Grady!" said Oliver.

Chapter Eight
Scramble

Two pirates followed O'Grady into
the anchor room. They began to pick up
the coils of rope from the floor.
The mice watched from their hiding place
by the crank.

"Caw." O'Grady's parrot flapped
his wings against the low ceiling.

"Yer right at that, Barney,"
grumbled O'Grady. "I'd rather be
up thar fillin' cats full o' cannon balls."
The ship shuddered and
groaned in the storm.

"Aw, quit it, O'Grady,"
mumbled Big Tom. "Somebody's
gotta tie down the sails."

"Any dumb sailor could do it—"

Big Tom interrupted. "Why then,
yer perfect for the job, now, ain't ya?
Har, har." He wagged his shaggy tail.

"Grrr," O'Grady snarled at him.
"If it warn't fer me an' Barney
'ere, the *Nine Lives* mighta
sailed away with the gold."

"Caw."

Big Tom heaved a coil of rope
around his shoulder. " 'Twas yer bird
that saw 'em. Not *you*.
I knows that fer sure."

He started up the ladder, then he called back down. "These waves er gettin' bigger, O'Grady.
Take a look at that anchor crank. Make sure it's good and sturdy afore ya comes up."

O'Grady growled. He set down his ropes and strutted over towards the anchor crank.

Oliver and Charles clutched at each other and crouched low.

Ker-thonk, ker-thonk.

Suddenly Oliver stood up straight. He darted right out toward O'Grady. Before the pirate had time to blink, Oliver had bitten his ankle.

"Yeow!" O'Grady hopped around on
his wooden leg, lost his balance,
and toppled to the floor. He glared at
the mouse. Oliver scampered for the doorway.

"Why, I'll tear ya limb from limb!"
The wild-eyed pirate leaped after Oliver.

Oliver scrambled away,
up the ladder, and onto the deck.
Barney flew after them.

Charles, left alone, gnawed harder
at the anchor rope. Oliver was buying him
some time. But what if they caught his friend?

Meanwhile, Oliver dashed
wildly around the deck with O'Grady
and Barney right behind him.

"I hates mice!" The pirate shouted
over the howling wind. "I *hates* 'em!"

Oliver leaped to the top of a pile
of cannonballs. Reckless now,
O'Grady ran right into them.

Thud! Clank! Bang!
Iron balls rolled all over the deck.
The ship pitched and tossed, and
the sea dogs tripped and fell
over each other.

"It's O'Grady! He's goin' mad!"
yelled Big Tom.

Oliver scurried onward, scrambling
up a rope toward the mast. Barney flew
up after him, but his master shouted,
"No, Barney, he's mine, all mine!"

O'Grady clamped his knife in
his teeth and climbed up the rigging.
His eyes glared. He slashed his knife
at the terrified mouse.

Oliver jumped out of the way and scrambled farther up. O'Grady kept climbing and slashing, cutting the ropes as he went.

"Stop 'im," yelled Big Tom. "He's goin' to rip the ship to shreds!" Three pirates climbed up after O'Grady.

But they were too late. O'Grady took one last stab, missed Oliver, and cut clean through the last rope of the rigging.

Snap! Thud!

Pirates, ropes, mouse, and sails crashed onto the deck. Captain Crag came bursting out of his cabin.

"Shiver me timbers, mates! Whose ship are we tryin' to sink here?"

"It's O'Grady. He's gone crazy!"
cried Big Tom to the captain.
The pirates sorted through
the pile of sailors and sails.

"O'Grady!" barked Crag. "What
got into ya?"

"It's the mouse, Cap'n!" panted
O'Grady. "That flea-bitten monster!
Where's he got to? I'll tear—"

Oliver lay half-dazed on the deck.
Captain Crag picked him up by the tail.
"This one here?"

O'Grady's eyes widened, and
he lunged toward the Captain.
Big Tom held him back.

"Easy now," said Crag.
"I'll take care of yer mouse."
The cruel bulldog chuckled.

Then he tied Oliver's tail
around his legs and stuck the mouse
in his pocket.

"Now you scalawags clean up yer mess
here," he growled. "An' resume fire
at the *Nine Lives*." He glared at
his crew.

Soon the cannons were blasting over
the waves again. The Captain strutted
back to his cabin and slammed the door
shut. He pulled Oliver out of his
pocket and tossed him onto the table.

"Oof!" Oliver landed hard.
He saw the model ship in the bottle
and tried to scramble up onto the window
ledge. Maybe he could hide—

But Oliver couldn't move.

"Har, har," laughed Crag. "I never seen such a fuss over a fat little mouse afore! Har, har, har."

Oliver trembled at the bulldog's laugh. Crag reached over and picked him up by his tied-up tail. He held the mouse close to his one good eye and stepped into the lantern light.

"Never ate a mouse afore," he mumbled. "But there's some meat on them bones." The old sea dog smiled a smile that sent chills to the tips of Oliver's whiskers.

Oliver tried to cry for help, but he was so scared that he couldn't even squeak. He stared into the bulldog's bloodshot eye. He felt more and more dizzy. Suddenly, he blacked out.

Chapter Nine
Sinking Fast

"Har, har, har." Captain Crag licked his chops. He was about to drop Oliver into his mouth when the ship lurched. The old bulldog fell halfway across his cabin.

He stumbled over to the table, still holding Oliver, and snatched up the bottled ship. He shoved Oliver inside. Then he corked the bottle shut and rushed off.

"What's up, mates?"

Frantic pirates scurried all over the deck. "She's cut loose, Cap'n!" yelled one.

"Well, blow me down," cried Crag. "Check the anchor, mates, on the double!"

Three dogs scrambled down into the hold. One frightened voice yelled back, "The rope be snapped, Cap'n. We lost the anchor!"

"Lost the anchor?" The Captain bellowed even louder than the wind. "Then find some way to stop her, mate—afore we be dashed to pieces on San Gato!"

Desperately the sea dogs tried to stop the *Herring Bone.* They tied ropes to cannons and heaved them overboard. But the waves were too strong. The rocky island came nearer and nearer.

"Prepare to abandon ship!" yelled the Captain. But no one heard him. A horrible sound of scraping wood came from below deck.

"We've hit!" shouted Big Tom. "She's takin' on water!"

Several sea dogs jumped overboard. The waves began to tear apart the *Herring Bone,* piece by piece. Planks began to grind and snap on the rocks beneath. Soon the sea would rush into the ship like a flood. It was every dog for himself.

Below deck, Charles was searching for his friend. "Oliver! Oliver!" he squeaked. But the crashing and splintering noises swallowed up his small voice.

He dodged as three wild-eyed
sea dogs dashed past him.
The foamy sea rushed after them.
Splash! The white water bowled Charles
over and covered him in a cold wave.

Suddenly he was riding the top of a
powerful wave that was filling the hold
with water. Just ahead was the ladder.
Charles reached up, grabbed one rung
of the ladder, and scampered up onto
the deck.

A roaring filled his ears. Charles
glanced over his shoulder. Another big
wave was about to hit the side of the
sinking ship. He snatched at a nearby
rope and held on tightly.
Water rushed over him.

After it had passed, he shook
himself and looked around.

Splintered masts, torn sails, and
tangled piles of rope littered the deck.
Not a sea dog was to be seen.
He braced himself against the rope
as another wave washed
over the ship.

"Oliver! Oliver!" he cried.
But the wind blew his words away.
Another wave smashed across the deck.

I've got to do something,
he thought. Or I'll go down with the ship.
But what about Oliver?

"Down with the ship?" he said
to himself. "The captain always goes
down with the ship. Doesn't he?
Maybe—if that old bulldog is still
in his cabin—maybe—even if he is a pirate—
maybe—he can tell me something
about Oliver."

Charles slipped and slid toward the captain's cabin. Moving a few feet at a time, he stopped to hang on whenever a wave washed over the deck. Finally the dripping mouse squeezed under the door into Crag's cabin.

The patch-eyed bulldog wasn't there.

Charles slumped onto the wet floor. "Oh, Oliver," he whispered. "Will I ever see you again, old friend?"

He heard a little squeak. At first he thought it was just the wind or a splintering board. He heard it again.

"Charles! Up here! It's me, Oliver!"

Charles stared up at the Captain's window ledge.

There was the bottle with the ship
in it. And in the bottle was a mouse
with his tail tied around his legs.

"Charles! Help me out of here!"
squeaked Oliver.

Charles scampered up onto the ledge
and tugged on the cork with all his might.

Pop! Charles rolled over
backwards with the cork in his paws.

"Oh, Charles!"

"Oh, Oliver!" Charles slid into
the bottle and untied his friend.

"Oh Charles!" Oliver shuddered.
"How are we going to get out of here?
We're going to go down with the ship."

Chapter Ten
Setting Sail

By midday the terrible storm had subsided. Sun leaked through the overcast sky, and the crew inspected their ship. Finally the *Nine Lives* set sail.

"She's weathered the storm pretty well, sir," said Mr. Calico.
"But I'm afraid we won't make it back to England. Not without some repairs. San Gato has plenty of trees for lumber—"

"—And a gang of dangerous shipwrecked sea dogs, as well."
The Admiral shook his head.
"We'll have to try for San Largo. Isn't that about twenty miles away?"

"Yes, sir. We might keep her afloat that long."

"Well, Mr. Calico, as they say, behind every cloud there's a silver lining. And we've had plenty of clouds lately." The Admiral smiled weakly. "Prepare to set sail for San Largo."

"Aye, aye, sir."

So Mr. Calico set to work with the rest of the crew. They mended sails, tied together broken masts and beams, and patched up holes.

Meanwhile, the storm melted away altogether. The evening sun broke through the clouds to the west over San Gato.

As the waves sparkled in the pink
sunset, Admiral Winchester stood
silently looking over the rail.
Even though the storm clouds had broken,
it seemed as if a cloud still hung
over his face.

Mr. Calico noticed the Admiral's
sad face and stepped over to his side.

"I'm feeling sorry about those
mice too, sir," he began. "They were
mighty brave little chaps—as mice go."

"Yes, they were," sighed Admiral
Winchester. "The Queen would have been
pleased to honor them. Maybe we can still
do something in memory of the heroic mice
of the *Herring Bone*." The Admiral
took off his hat and held it over his heart.

Mr. Calico stood quietly at his side for a moment. "Begging your pardon, sir," he said at last. "We're ready to lift anchor."

Admiral Winchester blinked. "Oh, yes. Of course, Mr. Calico. Set sail for San Largo at once." The Admiral replaced his hat and took one last look into the sunset.

"Wait a minute!"

Mr. Calico stopped. "Yes, sir?"

"Look, Mr. Calico!" Admiral Winchester pointed out across the flickering waves. "Do you see that?"

"See what, sir?"

"That—that *little ship*."

"*Little ship*, sir?"

"Yes!" The Admiral pointed again. "Right there. Do you see it, Mr. Calico?"

"Why, yes, sir. It's a little ship, it is."

The Admiral leaned over the railing. "Ahoy there!" he shouted. "Ahoy!"

"Ahoy!" piped back a very small voice.

Mr. Calico and the Admiral looked at each other in amazement.

"Ahoy!" repeated the voice from the little ship. "Admiral Winchester, the mice of the *Herring Bone* request permission to board ship."

"The mice of the *Herring Bone*?" Admiral Winchester's jaw dropped open.

Minutes later, the little ship had sailed up to the *Nine Lives*. Mr. Calico tossed a rope down to them.

Charles grabbed it and tied a square knot around the little ship's main mast. "Heave ho!" he called. "We're prepared to board!" And the little ship was pulled up onto the *Nine Lives*.

"It's the mice of the *Herring Bone*!" shouted the sailors to each other. Soon the whole ship was buzzing with excitement. All the cats gathered round to greet them.

"How on earth—?" began
Admiral Winchester.

"It wasn't easy,"
said Oliver.

"And it's a *long* story,"
added Charles.

"Perhaps a bite of cheese would help in the telling?" said Mr. Calico.

"No doubt," replied Oliver.

"As they say," chuckled the Admiral, "hungry as a mouse! Ha, ha." This time all the cats chuckled too. "Set sail for San Largo, mates. And now Mr. Calico and I have a story to hear!"

The crew pulled up anchor and set sail. Admiral Winchester and Mr. Calico took the mice with them to the Admiral's cabin. Charles and Oliver sat on the table before a chunk of fine Swiss cheese, ready to tell their tale.

The Admiral began. "There's one thing I'd like to know first, if you don't mind.

Just *where* did you
get that ship?"

Charles chuckled. "I'm sure
you've seen how they put model ships
in bottles, Admiral."

"Yes, I have."

"Well, we used this one, both
in the bottle and out of the bottle."

"Right!" Oliver joined in. "We
rode out the storm in the bottle until
it got washed up on shore."

"Then we broke the bottle and set
sail for the *Nine Lives* when the
weather calmed down," finished Charles.

"But where did you ever *get* it?"
Admiral Winchester still
sounded puzzled.

Charles smiled. "Why, didn't you notice the name on the side?"

"The *Herring Bone*," piped the two mice together.

"Well, I say," exclaimed the Admiral. "Captain Crag's own model!"

Oliver nibbled at the cheese, and Charles took a deep breath so he could begin their tale. But growls from outside interrupted him.

A voice snarled across the waves. "Ye ain't seen the last of us, ye flea-bitten cats!"

"Why, that sounds like Captain Crag," said Oliver, wide-eyed.

The Admiral got up and opened the window. The ship was passing by San Gato.

Captain Crag and several seaweed-covered dogs stood defiantly on the beach.

"We'll tear ya limb from limb!" howled the bulldog captain.

"We'll drown ya yet!" shouted O'Grady.

"I'll wring yer furry little necks!" barked Big Tom.

"Caw!" squawked Barney.

Admiral Winchester shut the window. "My, my." He settled himself back down. "Sounds as if they have a bone to pick with us, you might say."

"Yes, sir," replied Oliver. "It's probably a herring bone."

Charles, Admiral Winchester,
and even Mr. Calico grinned.
Oliver took another bite of cheese,
and the *Nine Lives* sailed off into the sunset.